eating peaches

Tara Heavey was born and raised in London, and moved to Dublin at the age of twelve. A qualified solicitor, she practised law in Co. Kilkenny and Co. Waterford for five years before turning to writing full-time. She lives in Co. Kilkenny with her partner and son.

Also by Tara Heavey

A Brush with Love

tara heavey

*eating
peaches*

PAN

First published 2004 by Tivoli,
an imprint of Gill & Macmillan, Dublin.

This edition published 2005 by Pan Books
an imprint of Pan Macmillan Ltd
20 New Wharf Road, London N1 9RR
Basingstoke and Oxford
Associated companies throughout the world
www.panmacmillan.com

ISBN 0 330 43315 6

A CIP catalogue record for this book is available from
the British Library.

Printed and bound in Great Britain by
Mackays of Chatham plc, Chatham, Kent

For Rory

Do I dare to eat a peach?

T.S. Eliot, 'The Love Song of J. Alfred Prufrock'

Prologue

Proper is my middle name. Well, it's really Bernadette. Elena Rose Bernadette Malone. My mother is a big fan of Russian ice-dancing. I got away lightly; my elder sister is called Tatiana. I used to call myself Elaine out of embarrassment. My friends call me Lainey out of kindness and affection.

Rose: that's where my beleaguered father came in. His mother's name.

Bernadette: enter the parish priest, horrified by the absence of a saint's name. If it hadn't been for the inclusion of Bernadette, he might have refused to baptise me. If not for the intercession of Saint

Bernadette, I could have been banished to the lower pits of hell for all eternity. Instead, here I stand, a good Irish Catholic girl with all the trimmings.

Malone. As in Molly.

But, anyway, Proper could have been my middle name. At least, that's what other people always seem to think. Imagine their surprise when they hear me swear for the first time. 'I never knew you cursed!' Expressions of amused shock on their faces – and a certain smugness: *Perhaps she's not perfect after all. Maybe humanity does lurk beneath that navy pinstripe and crisp white blouse.* Little do they know of the effing and blinding that goes on inside my head on an almost continuous basis. Especially when I'm talking to a client. No, I say. I can't believe your neighbour had the temerity to leave her bin out six inches over your boundary line! It's a national disgrace! Of course you shall have your day in court! The aromatic blend of curses and swear words that actually circles in my head doesn't find release until the client has been led safely down the corridor.

Because I'm a hypocrite. When you're a solicitor, being a hypocrite is an essential part of the job description. Hell, if you told the truth, you wouldn't have any clients left. Tell the punters what they want to hear and they'll come back for more. One must never burden one's client with the truth.

This attitude proved to be extremely good for business. I doubt it was very good for the soul. But, as I mentioned earlier, I had been baptised, so hopefully that earned me a few brownie points with the big guy upstairs.

Talking of the big guy upstairs, he had a few changes in store for me that I could never have anticipated.

I thought I'd always be sitting in my big, plush Dublin office, dealing with big, plush Dublin clients, and zipping around Dublin in my snazzy little sports car. Little did I know that I was due a major transformation.

Chapter One

I spun around on my new, luscious, black leather chair for what must have been the fortieth time that morning – and it wasn't even nine o'clock yet. Oh, how I loved the trappings of success! And if that made me a shallow person, so be it.

I was interrupted mid-spin by a knock on the door. I hastily readjusted my chair and picked up my fountain pen, as if poised to write something complicated and legalistic. I even furrowed my brow a little.

'Come in.'

In came Barb, my boss's secretary.

'Tyrone would like to see you, when you're ready.'

So you see, I wasn't the only one in the office with a funny name. My boss was called Tyrone Power. I kid you not. His mother, Mary, was a huge fan of the silver screen. Fifty-odd years before, she had married Michael Power of the county of Kilkenny. Tyrone maintains she married him solely so that she could inflict this terrible name on some poor unfortunate child – who happened to be him. He's always going on about changing it by deed poll, but what's the point in that when you're fifty-one years old? It would be like a man who's bald as a coot walking into the office one day sporting a thick black rug on his head.

Not that Tyrone is bald. He has a head of lush silver hair, and liquid brown eyes. He's a little on the portly side, but he's tall and carries it well. It almost suits him; he takes up more space in the courtroom. He's intense – frightening, if you don't know him. All the young secretaries are terrified of him, especially when he lets out one of his famous lion-roars. But that's just a sound effect. Gets things done.

Tyrone and I saw through each other from the outset. He baited me mercilessly when he inter-viewed me for my apprenticeship; cross-examined me, trying every trick in his very long book to make me lose my cool. But I could see that he was a softie deep down, and I held it all together. Hard to believe that had been almost seven years ago.

And this morning he wanted to see me about something.

I hardly dared guess that this was the moment I had been waiting for. Tyrone had been hinting for some time that partnership was imminent. I already had the plush office, the luxurious company car. I knew that he was pleased with me. Surely the next logical step....

'Come in and sit down, Lainey.'

Lainey. That was a good sign. 'Elena' was reserved for company and the odd bollocking. He swivelled his swively chair around to face me, leaned back and yawned. The bags under his eyes were like miniature hammocks and his shirt was crumpled. The top button was undone and his tie veered to the left. He looked like he'd put in an all-nighter.

'Have you been here all night?'

'No, just got in.'

What was wrong with this picture?

He continued to observe me until I started to fidget.

'You wanted to see me about something, Tyrone.'

'Yes, that's right, I did.'

Still nothing.

Then: 'You'll have some coffee?' He didn't wait for my reply, just buzzed the order out to Barb. I was slightly concerned. Evasive was not this man's middle name (I think it could have been Francis).

'Is there something wrong?'

He got up and stood looking out of the window, leaning like a corner boy, hands deep in his pockets.

The view was of the canal. Dublin pedestrians and cars scurried by like insects.

'I haven't been very well lately.'

A distant alarm bell started to ring.

'Oh?' I said profoundly.

'My doctor thinks I should slow down a little. No more working weekends, late nights, all that.'

'Nothing serious, I hope.'

He swatted the comment away like a pesky fly. 'No, no, not at all. Just too much stress, high blood pressure, that sort of thing.'

I nodded. That sounded all right. Didn't it?

'Can I do anything to help? Take on some of your files? You just have to ask.'

He turned to me and smiled warmly. 'Actually, I do need a favour.'

'Go on.'

'I'm thinking of moving back down the country.'

You what!

My racing thoughts were interrupted by a sharp rap on the door and the entrance of Barb. She gave me a digestive biscuit, a hot coffee and a cold stare. I noticed that Tyrone got a chocolate digestive while mine was plain. Barb didn't dislike me in particular; she just hated any female who came within a ten-foot radius of her beloved Tyrone. She was about ten years his senior, but this didn't seem to hinder her crush. The younger secretaries called her Miss Moneypenny behind her back, when they weren't calling her Barbed Wire. Tyrone just seemed

9

oblivious. If anyone asked him for his opinion of her, he told them that she was a damn good secretary.

Tyrone sat down heavily and reached into a side drawer, pulling out a pack of Benson & Hedges and a solid gold lighter. Barb, who had been about to close the door behind her, flew back to his desk as if aided by supernatural powers (come to think of it ... invisible broomstick?).

'What do you think you're doing?' She bore down on him like a Fury, hands on hips, spitting fire. Jesus, she was one scary woman. Tyrone held up his hands as if he were under arrest and let the box of cigarettes fall like an illegal firearm.

'By God, woman! Is a man to have no peace in his own office?' He tried to make a joke out of it, but his calculated rakish grin failed to dent her steely demeanour.

'Give them to me.' She held out one hand, arm rigid; the other remained firmly on her matronly hip. She reminded me of a strict schoolmistress confiscating a contraband sweet or an illicit note. Sulkily, he handed her the cigarettes.

'And the lighter.'

'Oh, come on, Barb –'

'Now! You're not to be trusted. You know well what the doctor said.'

He handed over the lighter, for all the world like an overgrown bold child.

Her voice and manner softened somewhat. 'You can have some of that special chewing gum I got you.'

'Don't want any.'

She turned on her heel, tutting and shaking her head as she went.

I waited until she had gone before I said anything. I wasn't that stupid.

'Isn't she afraid that you'll stick a piece of gum under your desk and make a terrible mess?'

'Don't start.'

'She's not in a very good mood. Did you forget to bring her in an apple this morning?'

'Yeah, yeah. Very funny, I'm sure. Now can we drop it, please? You didn't see that, okay?'

'Okay. So what else did the doctor say?' I tried to keep the concern out of my voice.

'That if I don't quit this job I'll be dead within three years.'

I was silent. Tyrone didn't say anything either; he just stared at me hard, trying to gauge my reaction. I was aware of the scrutiny and struggled not to let any emotion show. *Stay calm, Lainey.*

After a while, I said, 'But, Tyrone … this job is your life.' Okay, not very comforting, but the truth. Tyrone had no wife and no kids. He had built the practice up from scratch. Now he had fifteen solicitors working for him and was one of the most respected lawyers in the city. If it didn't sound like such a cliché I'd say that the firm was his family.

'Well, I'm not going to give it up altogether. I'm going to open a sub-office back home and run that instead. The pace of life is slower down there, and I can take it a lot easier.'

'Do you think you can be happy doing that?'

'I think so. I've been hankering for home a lot recently. In fact, I quite fancy myself as a country squire.'

I had a disturbing mental image of Tyrone in an old-fashioned tweed suit, shotgun tucked under his arm, trouser legs tucked into his socks, a couple of dead rabbits slung across his shoulder. I shuddered – especially at the vision of his matching tweed hat with flaps over the ears.

'When are you going?'

'As soon as I can. I estimate it'll take me about nine months to wind down here and hand over the reins. That's where you come in.'

He surely didn't mean that he was going to hand over the reins to me? There were plenty of more senior solicitors in the firm. I felt a knot of excitement begin to tighten in my stomach all the same.

'I need someone to head down before me, to get the ball rolling. The premises are all sorted. A new housing estate is just being completed; the auctioneer is my first cousin, and he's promised to send plenty of business my way....'

I wasn't listening any more. The knot in my stomach was unravelling. Surely he didn't mean …

'... So you'd only need to be there for about nine months....'

'What?'

'I'll need you down there for about nine months, while I honour my commitments here. You can stay in the old family home. Rent-free!'

Big swinging mickies, I thought. *What's in it for me?*

'I suppose you're wondering what's in it for you.'

'I wasn't, I –'

Tyrone laughed at me. 'It's all right. I don't blame you.' He stood and faced me, beefy hands (they were farmer's hands. Why hadn't I noticed before?) leaning on the desk. His eyes blazed into mine. The bastard was enjoying this.

'If you do this for me, there's a partnership in it for you at the end of the nine months.'

Now you're talking.

'And if I don't do it?'

'There's plenty more out there who'd jump at the opportunity.'

'All right. I get it. I'll do it. When do I have to go?'

'Two weeks' time.'

Holy shit.

'Okay. Where exactly am I going, anyway?'

'You, my dear Elena, are destined for the throbbing metropolis of Ballyknock.'

Chapter Two

I thought Christiana was going to rupture something.

'Ballymuck? You're making it up!'

'It's Ballyknock. I'm not saying it again.'

'Ballymuck!'

This time I thought she was going to explode, she was laughing so hard. I tried not to let my annoyance show. This really wasn't helping.

'This really isn't helping, you know.'

'Sorry, sorry. Just give me a minute to compose myself.' She wiped a tear from her eye with the back of her hand and made an obvious attempt to compose her features. After a while, her face lost some of its redness and returned to its normal pinky-white hue.

'Where exactly is it, then?' Hazel asked.

'In the heart of the Kilkenny countryside.'

'In the middle of nowhere, like.'

'In the middle of nowhere.'

'Cows and fields.'

'Cows and fields.'

'How far to the nearest shop?'

'Five miles.'

'How far to the nearest pub?'

'Five miles.'

'Fucking hell!' they chorused.

'You won't last two weeks,' Hazel said helpfully.

'Jesus, girls, would you give me some credit? It's only for nine months, and I'm neither a shopaholic nor an alcoholic.' I washed this sentence down with a generous gulp of Chianti.

'Nine months. That's how long it takes for a baby to grow,' Christiana informed us solemnly. Then her eyes widened in shocked excitement.

'That's it, isn't it? You're pregnant!' She pounced on the idea like a cat on a mouse. 'You don't want anyone to know, so you're going down to the arse-hole of nowhere, where nobody knows you, and you're going to have the child in secret, and then it'll be adopted by a rich doctor and his kindly wife who can't have any children of their own.' The words came tumbling out.

'Yes, Chris. I'm really going to work in a laundry run by evil nuns who'll whip me if I don't wash their drawers quickly enough. Then they'll refuse

15

to let me have an epidural during labour, to punish me for my sins, and then they're going to wrench the newborn infant from my arms and give it to a God-fearing Catholic family.'

'I knew it!'

'Chris, have you been reading that book about the Magdalene Laundries again? Remind me to confiscate it,' said Hazel, rolling her eyes at me.

'The most fertile thing around here is your imagination, Chris. It's not the 1950s.'

'So you're really just going down there to work as a solicitor, then?'

'Of course.'

'Oh.' She sounded so disappointed that I was almost tempted to make up an elaborate lie for her benefit.

Hazel and Christiana were my flatmates. It was the evening after Tyrone had delivered his shock news, and we were sitting around the coffee table in what we laughingly called 'the good room'. It was only 8.30 p.m., post-*EastEnders*, but the second bottle of wine had already been opened. We three sat curled up on the overstuffed couch, engulfed in a haze of cigarette smoke and alcohol fumes. It was an all-too-common scenario.

Christiana was pretty well twisted already. This partly accounted for the excessive giggling and wild theories – but not totally. Her friends described her as 'off-beat' or 'a little off the wall'. If she'd had any enemies, which I sincerely doubted, they probably

would have described her as 'completely barking'.
Hazel and I were her friends – although how and
why Hazel and Christiana were friends was anybody's guess. Chalk and cheese weren't in it. In fact,
just to illustrate my point, I'm going to set out
their differences in tabulated form. I like doing this
sort of thing. It must have something to do with
being a lawyer.

Christiana	Hazel
Ditzy	Salt of the earth
Too much to say	Woman of few words
Gullible	Cynical
Easily led	Leading easily
Believed in ghosts	Believed that anyone who believed in ghosts should be committed forthwith

Christiana worked 'in film'. Nobody – including
Christiana herself – was quite sure what she did,
but she seemed to be paid an awful lot of money
for it. Hazel was an accountant by name and by
nature. As the Americans would say, go figure.

Christiana fell in love with a different person
every single week. She claimed she was bisexual, but
I suspected this was only because it was currently
fashionable in the film industry – I think it was
Drew Barrymore who had started this particular
trend. Quite frankly, I had difficulty keeping track.
On a weekly basis, extravagant bunches of flowers

were delivered to the flat with her name on them. It was quite annoying, actually. They were usually from some new, up-and-coming director or from a bit-part actor or actress. These relationships tended to last roughly as long as the flowers. Either Chris blew them off because of their lack of 'Heathcliff-like qualities' (her words, not mine) or they realised in the nick of time that she had fallen off her trolley a long time ago. Hazel, on the other hand, was resolutely single. She hadn't got where she was with the aid of a man, no sirree Bob. In her opinion, a husband was a sign of weakness.

I was the only one with a steady boyfriend. Steady being the operative word.

Paul was an accountant too. He worked in the same office as Hazel, and we had hooked up at one of their work do's (or should I say work don'ts). It had been a total set-up. Paul had been taken under the wing of his best friend's newly appointed wife. Having sorted out her own love life, she turned her attention to the so-called love lives of others for her entertainment. She was Paul's social secretary. Hazel was my marketing manager. Wifey decided that I would be perfect for Paul, as I was a solicitor and therefore bound to be sensible and financially viable. How wrong can you be?

'What does Paul think?' asked Hazel.

'I haven't told him yet. I'm seeing him tomorrow night.'

Hazel nodded but was silent. I could tell that she

was worried. She suspected that all was not rosy in the Paul–Lainey garden. I guessed she was just saying nothing and keeping her fingers crossed that it would all work out. Otherwise, how was she going to take credit for our wedding?

'We'll have to have a going-away do!' It was Chris, squealing with excitement yet again.

'Oh, no. The last thing I want is a big fuss.'

'But we can't let you go off to Ballymuck without a proper send-off.'

'For the last time – Ballyknock!'

'Whatever. Go on. Say yes!'

'Oh, all right, then, if it'll get you off my back.'

'Yes!'

'But you'll have to keep it small. You, me, Hazel and Paul. You're not to invite any of your loony friends.'

'I won't, I promise. Just leave it all to me and I'll arrange everything. You're not going to regret this, Lainey.'

One small tip: whenever anyone says those words to you, start worrying.

Paul thrust inside me as if he were trying to push a boulder up a hill. I wished fervently that he'd reach the summit and hoist his flag. *How much longer?* His face hovered inches above my own, ghostly white. Beads of sweat had begun to form on his forehead. I watched in fascination as his features contorted and his body shuddered.

'Oh God!'

Thank God.

Paul collapsed on top of me. I lay beneath his sweaty bulk, waiting for a decent interval to expire before I could push him off. I judged ten seconds to be an adequate period.

'Paul,' I said gently, and patted him on the shoulder. He grunted in reply.

'Paul. I need to use the bathroom.'

'Oh, yeah, right…. Sorry.' Assisted by what I hoped seemed like a gentle shove, he rolled off me onto the other side of the bed. I leapt up enthusiastically, padded naked into the bathroom and locked the door, relieved to be on my own. I viciously spun the toilet-roll holder, releasing far more squares of toilet paper than I actually needed. *That'll teach him*, I thought unreasonably. Paul was a two-squares-only man, for both economic and environmental reasons. *Fuck the environment and fuck him.* I wiped away the meagre juices that my body had produced due to his ministrations and flushed angrily, watching with satisfaction as the toilet swallowed all evidence of our brief encounter.

As I washed my hands, I looked up into the mirror and sighed. I smoothed down my long blonde hair. We're not talking Pamela Anderson here; more Lady Helen Taylor – the type of hair that looks well adorned with an Alice band or swept back into a sleek chignon. People thought it was classy. I looked for a brush or comb in vain. Paul didn't have much use for them, being an advocate of the Phil Mitchell school of hairdressing, and I didn't dare leave my own hairbrush in his bathroom in case he thought I was dropping hints about moving in with him. He panicked at the mere presence of a carelessly discarded earring on his bedside table.

I scrutinised my face in the mirror. That was never a crow's foot at the outer corner of my left eye? It couldn't be. I was only twenty-nine and a bit. Since my last birthday I had developed an all-consuming obsession with crow's feet, laughter lines and any other facial inconsistency remotely resembling a wrinkle. I often snuck up on my reflection unexpectedly, trying to catch any lurking lines unawares. And, to add insult to injury, I still got the odd spot. Surely that wasn't on, having to worry about pimples and wrinkles simultaneously? It was like seeing a dead leaf on a glorious summer day.

There was definitely a dry patch on my right cheek. I opened the bathroom cabinet, searching for some kind of moisturiser to remedy the situation. Paul's lotions and potions were lined up like little plastic soldiers. It was most definitely a boy's bathroom. Not a hint of pink or a gently curved shape anywhere; all the containers were either dark blue or metallic grey and were shaped like phallic symbols, as if the advertisers were trying to reassure the male consumer that, no, you're not a poof if you buy exfoliator. All those little lines of plastic penises arranged with pathological neatness. Freaky.

'Lainey, are you going to be long in there? I'm dying for a pee.'

I slammed the cabinet door. I couldn't get a moment's peace.

'I'm coming.' *For the first time tonight*, I felt like adding.

Paul stood on the other side of the door, grinning sheepishly and shifting from one bare foot to the other. He was clutching his privates in one hand and holding a full condom in the other. We come bearing gifts. I was exposed in the fluorescent glare of the harsh bathroom light. I felt my dimpled thighs did not bear scrutiny. So what if I didn't know whether I fancied him any more? It was still important that he should find me attractive. I dodged Paul's kiss as I slunk by him into the safety of the dimly lit bedroom.

I would have killed for a fag, but Paul would have gone berserk if I'd lit up in his precious bedroom. The last time I had tried it he had thrown the offending item out of the open window – fully lit! How inconsiderate. He could have caused a forest fire or anything.

I could hear him banging around in the kitchen now, opening and closing presses. The kettle hissed reassuringly in the background. A few minutes later Paul emerged, clad only in a pair of gingham boxer shorts, bearing a tray heavy with teapot, milk carton and plate of warm buttered toast. He smiled shyly at me as he placed the tray on the rumpled bed. He reminded me of a little boy bringing his mammy breakfast on Mothers' Day.

'I thought you might have the munchies.' He began pouring me a cup of tea, milk first, just the way I liked it. I felt sick with shame at my earlier mean thoughts. I'd forgotten how lovely he could be at times. I almost remembered why I'd gone out with him in the first place.

I examined his face as I bit into my first slice of toast. Regular, classically handsome features: light-hazel eyes, soft brown hair, strong nose, full firm mouth, and cheekbones that a supermodel would be proud of. So why did I feel so irritated every time I looked at him nowadays? He could be great when he wanted to be. And he had so obviously wanted to be tonight. It was just all the other times – when he didn't want to be great – that were the problem.

There was the excessive tidiness, for a start. It had seemed like a joke at the beginning, an endearing quirk – part of his charm, if you like. CDs arranged in alphabetical order; socks and jocks stored in colour-coordinated bundles, neatly rolled and folded. And then there was the obsession with hygiene. Germs! Everywhere! It was just so … well, it was downright anal, to tell the truth. I had reached the end of my rope with it some time ago; I had tied a knot on the end and I was hanging on for dear life.

I suppose it wouldn't have been so bad if I had also been a neat freak. It might have been a big plus. But not only was I not a neat freak, I wasn't even averagely tidy. In fact, I was a slob – albeit a secret slob. My colleagues would probably never have guessed. I kept my office in reasonably good nick. And I was always well turned out: suits regularly dry-cleaned, shoes and nails polished, hair groomed, face done. My flatmates knew all about it, though. They were as bad as me. That was why I rarely brought Paul around to the flat. I was afraid he'd faint. When left to my own devices, I could literally fester in my juices for days. My tolerance for dirt was astounding. And as for germs … you couldn't even see them, therefore they didn't exist.

And then, God help us, there was the sex – or lack thereof, as we might say in the legal world. Not that it made much difference; I could have slept through most of our sessions nowadays. There was nothing wrong with Paul's technique, as such. It was just that I was never allowed any input. Paul had to call all of the shots all of the time. I was at screaming point there, too.

My family were convinced that we were going to announce the tying of the knot any day now. They were in for a rude awakening.

I decided to bite the bullet as well as the toast.

'Paul, I have something to tell you.'

The hand bringing the mug to his lips froze in mid-air. 'You're not pregnant, are you?'

'No, I'm not pregnant!'

Relief flooded his face, and he took a sip of tea.

Jesus. Where had that come from? Had I gotten really fat lately or something? And how on earth did he think I could possibly get pregnant, what with him being so acutely careful all of the time? He wouldn't even hear of me going on the pill, probably because he didn't trust me to take it. He was the only man I knew who relished using condoms. That way he could ensure that he was in complete control. His sperm didn't stand a chance. At least it eliminated fights about who got to sleep on the wet patch.

Perverse as I knew it was, I felt secretly jealous whenever I heard of a couple getting pregnant by accident. I could only dream about the kind of passion that would result in bringing a love-child into this world – forgetting all about the tearing of condom wrappers and the balling of socks. Oh, the oblivion of torn tights!

'I have to go away for a while.'

'Define "go away".'

I told him, watching his reaction carefully. His expression remained blank. He kept his eyes down-cast throughout. Just kept right on sitting there at the edge of the bed. Topless. Five o'clock shadow – now nine o'clock shadow. Rough. My favourite version of Paul.

'Well?' The suspense was too much.

He raised his eyes slowly to mine.

'Would you like me to go with you?'

That was unexpected.

'Don't be daft. You have your job to think about; and it's only for nine months. We can still see each other at weekends – if you like.'

'Of course I like,' he said quickly. He took my hand without looking at me and stroked it gently with the ball of his thumb. He whispered something I couldn't quite catch.

'What was that?'

'I'll miss you, Lainey.'

My heart melted a little and I felt a curious mixture of affection, irritation and guilt. I thought that I should say something in return.

'Will you miss me too?'

That was it. That was what I was meant to say. 'Of course I'll miss you,' I said quickly. I almost meant it, too. In fairness, I was in shock. Paul wasn't the most demonstrative of men; this was pretty soul-revealing stuff for him.

'When did you say you were going, again?'

'In a little under two weeks.'

'So you'll be away for our anniversary.'

Another bolt from the blue. In a few weeks' time, Paul and I would have been going out for exactly one year. I remembered the date, but I was amazed that he had. We hadn't even discussed it. I fixed a smile on my face to hide the shock. 'Never mind. We can still do something special.'

Paul had stopped talking. I looked up and noticed

26

that he was staring at my left breast, which had popped out of its hiding-place behind the duvet. I cleared my throat uncomfortably and pulled the covers up to my chin.

'I'd better be going,' I said, hopping out of bed and quickly grabbing my clothes.

'Why don't you stay the night?'

'No. I didn't bring clean underwear, and besides, I have an early start….' I was already half-dressed.

'When will I see you again?' Paul called out to me as I was halfway out the door.

'I'll give you a call.'

I put off phoning home for as long as possible. Finally it became so uncomfortable that it was easier just to do it.

'Hi, Dad.'

'That you, Rosie?' My dad refuses on principle to call me by my first name. It infuriates my mother. It's meant to.

'Yeah, it's me. Listen, Dad, I have some news.'

'You're getting married.'

'For the last time, no!' I almost shouted.

'All right, all right. No need to get your knickers in a twist. I was only saying. You are nearly thirty now, you know.'

'Thanks for reminding me.'

'And someone has to carry on the family line. We've given up on your sister.' Tatiana (we called her Annie) was thirty-four years old and single. I didn't know which was worse, being branded as the family brood mare or as a lost cause.

'Hello, dear.' It was my mother on the other line.

'Hi, Mum. Look, I'm glad I've got you both together. Something's happened in work.'

'You've been made a partner?'

'Not exactly, but it's in the offing.' I explained the situation.

'But, Rosie, you hate the countryside.'

'Do not.'

'Yes, you do,' they exclaimed together.

Both of my parents are from the West. Childhood family holidays consisted of driving through somewhere like Connemara, past acres of fields, sheep, dry stone walls, rocks, more sheep and more rocks. The monotony was broken only by stop-offs in lay-bys, where we ate limp Calvita-and-Tayto sandwiches – which tasted to us like manna from heaven – washed down with warm, flat 7-Up and a flask of tepid tea. Then we'd examine dolmens, piles of rocks assembled by our ancient forefathers to commemorate dead chieftains. High excitement for a couple of pre-pubescent city chicklets.

'Admire the rocks!' Dad would exclaim angrily. 'They were put there by your ancestors.' And Annie and I would wonder why our ancestors couldn't have found something more productive to do with their time.

And then there was the rain, the incessant, driving rain. I shuddered, recalling weeks spent shivering in a caravan in the middle of a field in County Roscommon. The sun would refuse to come out until we got back to Dublin. My sister and I would run out of the car straight to our friends' houses, with tall tales about freckled Mayo boys who had looked at us funny, leaving our deflated parents to shake their heads at their repeated failure to educate their daughters about their cultural heritage.

But that had been years ago. I was sure I must have developed some appreciation for the countryside in the meantime. And if I hadn't, it was about time I did.

'Well, I for one think you're doing the right thing, Elena. It's a wonderful opportunity for you – and, besides, you owe it to Tyrone. He's always been very good to you.'

'Thanks, Mum.'

'Where did you say you'll be living again?' asked Dad.

'In Tyrone's old family home. It's a little cottage in the middle of nowhere, apparently.'

'When you say "middle of nowhere", what do you mean exactly? Do you have any neighbours?'

'I think there's a couple of houses close by.'

'And you're going to be living there on your own?'

'Of course.'

'Is there an alarm on the house?'

'I don't think so. Why would there be? It's in the middle of nowhere. And there's nothing to take, anyway.'

'There's *you* to take! Merciful hour, Rosie, you're not staying there on your own. You'll be murdered to death.'

'Dad!'

'You hear about it every day. Young women living in isolated country cottages, murdered in their own beds. Or worse.'

'Don't mind him, Elena. You'll be grand. You can get yourself a nice big dog to protect you.'

'But you know I don't like dogs, Mum.'

'Nonsense. You've always loved dogs. And it'll be great company for you, if nothing else. We'll go down to the pound next week and pick you out something suitable.'

'It's a dog, Mum, not a handbag.'

Oh, what was the use?

'Anyway, I've got to go. I'm only in the door and I have an early start in the morning.'

'It's ten o'clock! Where have you been all this time?'

'I was just out with the girls.' I was hardly going to admit to having unsatisfying, unmarried sex with my boyfriend. 'I'll talk to you both soon.'

'Goodbye, Elena. Sleep well.'

'Night, Rosie.'

I sighed with relief as I put down the phone. That was everyone important told.

Now I just had to get used to the idea myself.

Chapter Three

That was that, then: last day in the Dublin office for at least another nine months. It had taken me most of Saturday to tie up loose ends, so it was well after six by the time I let myself into the apartment that I'd called home for three years and three rent-hikes. I had decided to keep my room. It made sense: I was only going to be in Ballyknock temporarily, and I planned to come to Dublin every weekend anyhow. I knew I should probably do the sensible thing and look for a place of my own to buy. But I loved living there.

'Hello! Anybody home?'

No reply. Perhaps they hadn't heard me. Perhaps this was because Björk was caterwauling at the top of her lungs. Christiana was blaring her latest CD at full volume. It was her customary getting-into-the-party-mood music. She played it a lot. We'd be getting another snotty letter from the landlord if she wasn't careful.

I pushed open the door of the living room. Hazel was sitting at the table with her back to me, hunched over a bunch of official-looking papers.

'Not working weekends again?'

No response.

I went up behind her and spoke into her left ear. 'I said, you're not work—'

'Jesus Christ!' Hazel jumped as if she'd been scalded, and her Biro went flying across the room. She slumped with relief when she saw it was me.

'Lainey! You frightened the shite out of me. What are you doing here?'

'I live here, remember? God, you're on edge. Been overdosing on the caffeine again?'

'What?'

'I said it looks like —'

'Oh, hold on.' Hazel removed a lump of Blu-tac from each ear. 'For fuck's sake. A person can't hear herself think, let alone work, with that Icelandic witch wailing in the background. I've already asked Chris to turn it down twice.'

'Give her a break. She probably doesn't expect anyone to be working at home on a Saturday evening. Which brings me to my next point: what's with all the paperwork?'

'Don't be talking. We've got a major deal going down in work. My ass is really on the line with this one, Lainey. I wouldn't be going out tonight if it wasn't ...'

'If it wasn't my going-away? Go on; you can say it. I don't mind. In fact, I'm thrilled to be the cause of you taking a break. Anyway, what about that boss of yours? I don't suppose he's working the weekend.'

'That bastard! You must be joking. Golf in Killarney again.'

'You should tell him where to go, Hazel. He's really taking the piss.'

'I know, but it's only temporary. Things will calm down once this deal is through.'

'Until the next deal. You've been saying that ever since you started working there. It's never going to calm down. Can't you see that? You work all the hours God sends, and you're never on top of things.' I peered over her shoulder at the rows and rows of minute figures. 'I don't know how you and Paul don't go cross-eyed looking at all those numbers.'

A persistent thudding was now emanating from the general direction of Christiana's bedroom.

'What *is* she up to in there?'

'God knows. Probably "creating" new dance routines. She could be committing hara-kiri for all I care.' Hazel sounded really annoyed.

'Deary me. Is she still getting on your nerves a little?'

'A little! It's like living with a cross between

Bubbles from *Ab Fab* and Samantha from *Sex and the City*. She never stops. She's driving me demented.'

'But she's always like that.'

'Yeah, I know. I just dread to think what it's going to be like with you gone all week. You're like the buffer. It's not as – I don't know – not as intense when there are three of us. I need another person to help take the strain.'

'I didn't realise you felt this way. Is it really that bad?'

'Worse. I'm thinking about looking for my own place.'

'No way!'

Hazel nodded wearily.

'But you've known each other since you were six.'

'I know.'

'You sat beside each other all through school.'

'Only because our surnames start with the same letter. It wasn't by choice.'

'But you've told me a million times how you braided each other's hair and bought gobstoppers together and swapped marbles –'

'Yeah. And then she lost her marbles.'

'But I don't understand. She lost them years ago. She's your best friend.' Along with me, I hoped.

'Used to be my best friend. I don't know, Lainey. I think we've just grown apart.'

'I'm sure it's just a phase,' I said hopefully. I didn't want our cosy little set-up to change. 'And I'll be back in a few months to help smooth things over.'

'Yeah, maybe.' Hazel didn't look or sound convinced.

Talk of the devil....

'Hazel, will you help me put my fake tan on ... Lainey! You're here!' Christiana burst through the door and ran over to me, flinging her arms around my neck. 'I didn't hear you come in.'

'*Quelle surprise*,' Hazel muttered under her breath, just loud enough for us both to hear.

'I'm only here a few minutes.'

'Hazel, this is what I thought you could wear tonight.' Chris waved a wisp of shocking-pink material in front of Hazel's face. Believe it or not, this constituted an entire outfit – a skirt and top, to be precise. It wasn't exactly what I would have described as Hazel's style.

'Would you ever fuck off with yourself? I'm not wearing *that*.'

'But I wore it last week and it was lovely on me.'

'Well, *I* don't want to look like a tart.'

'Hazel!' I was shocked. I'd never heard her speak that way to Chris before. But I was ignored: Hazel stomped out of the room, roughly pushing past Chris.

Jesus! Things were worse than I'd thought.

'Don't mind Hazel,' I said gently. 'She's just been working too hard. I mean, look at that.' I gestured to the pile of papers on the table. 'On Saturday night, of all nights. I mean, it's just ridiculous.'

Christiana nodded vacantly.

'Did you say you needed some help with your fake tan?'

Chris silently handed me the bottle of Clarins spray (the best fake tan there was, in her expert opinion) that she had been clutching, and sat on one of the stools at the breakfast bar.

'Where do you want it?'

'On my back.' She pulled her top over her head and slipped out of her bra. She was as unselfconscious as a child. I started spraying the tan on her shoulders and rubbing it in.

'What are you wearing tonight, Chris?'

'My new Whistles jumper.'

I thought about this for a few seconds. 'But that means nobody will be able to see your back.'

'That doesn't matter. I'll know it's there.'

'Oh.' My friend the fake-tan junkie. 'You know, pet, if you had a baby it would come out orange.'

'Yeah? Do you think it would have ginger hair, too?'

'Most definitely.'

'That's good. I love red hair.'

She got distracted then; drifted off into one of her daydreams. Who knew what went on in that girl's head? I retreated into my own little world, and for a few minutes all was quiet between the rubber and the rubbee. Until:

'Lainey, I have something to tell you.'

I stopped rubbing. 'What?'

'You know how I said I'd arrange your going-away?'

36

'Yes.' My gut told me that this wasn't going to be good.

'And you know how you said it was just to be you, me, Haze and Paul?'

'Chris, what have you done?'

'Well – I might have invited a few extra people along by mistake.'

'How can you invite people by mistake?'

'It just sort of slipped out.'

'How many?'

'One or two.'

'How many?'

'Six.'

'Six! For pity's sake, Chris. Who are they?'

She reeled off a list of names that made me immediately lose my appetite. I could have clocked her one. Undaunted, she alighted on a new topic.

'What are you wearing tonight?'

'I hadn't really thought.'

'Oooh. You can borrow something of mine if you like.'

'No, thank you.' If I'd wanted to look like a clown I would have joined the circus.

'Oh, go on. It'll be fun.' Fun for her, maybe. Apart from inventing appalling dance routines, Christiana's main hobby was doing people up. When she was a little girl, her favourite toy had been Girl's World. The reason I knew this was that she still had it in her room. Some people might have jumped at this opportunity for a free

make-over. I, however, had seen some of her previous victims.

'No, Chris. I've got plenty of perfectly good
clothes of my own.'

'But your clothes are so boring. You need to use
your imagination more when you dress.'

'I'm not supposed to have an imagination. I'm a
solicitor.'

'You need to express yourself more.'

'By that you mean show more flesh.'

'If I had your chest I'd show it off all the time.
Oh, let me pick your outfit, please! Think of it as
an extra-special going-away present from me to
you. Oh please, please, please!'

I looked down at her upturned little face, devoid
of make-up, devoid of artifice. I thought of how
hurt she must have been by Hazel's behaviour,
though she had tried so hard not to show it.

'Okay. But just the top.' What was I letting
myself in for?

'Oh, brilliant!' She clapped her hands gleefully,
jumped off the stool and ran to the door. 'Oh – are
you finished my back?'

'One back fully tanned.' I was already washing
my hands at the kitchen sink, although I knew
that, whatever I did, they'd be tangerine later on
that night.

'You won't regret this,' I heard her calling from
the hall.

I was regretting it already.

I spent the next half-hour trying on at least fifty different tops, each one more outrageous than the last. Finally we agreed on a wine-coloured angora cardigan, trimmed around the neck and down the centre with what looked like feathers in varying shades of wine and pink. It was lower-cut than I was used to, but I could live with that. Chris wanted me to wear it with all the buttons open, except for one at the chest, and nothing underneath. It was all right for her, with her toned midriff and pierced belly button; I was a mere mortal, with a roll of fat to keep in check. A matching wine camisole was debated over and decided upon.

I had to fight for the right to wear my own dressy black trousers and flat black boots. Christiana was most insistent on a pair of fake-snakeskin boots with four-inch spike heels. I won that particular dispute by giving a very convincing demonstration of my inability to walk in them. Chris herself was an expert at walking in high heels; at five foot one and three-quarters, she never wore heels lower than three inches. She was like a white, female version of The Artist Currently Known as Squiggle.

Once I had dispatched Chris to her room to complete her own extensive titivations, I rapped gingerly on Hazel's door.

'Who is it?'

'It's me.'

'Come in.'

She was sitting cross-legged on her bed, reading a book and dressed in her all-black going-out uniform. She looked up as I entered.

'She never got you to wear one of her tops!' She shook her head. 'I can't believe you were so spineless.'

'It's not a question of being spineless. I was trying to cheer her up. She was upset.'

Hazel didn't reply.

'Besides, I got away lightly. You should have seen some of the stuff she was trying to get me into.'

'I believe you.'

I sat down on the bed beside her. 'I suppose you knew about those twats coming along tonight.'

'Sorry about that. I was sworn to secrecy.'

'Are you ready, then?'

'I'm not going.'

'Well, how come you're dressed to go out?'

I could see her trying to think of an answer. 'I got dressed and then I changed my mind.'

'Well, change it back. Seriously, Hazel, surely you're not going to miss this golden opportunity to take the piss out of Chris's friends? It'll be a laugh. Besides, I'll need someone normal to talk to. You can't abandon me like this. It's like throwing a Christian to the lions.'

'I wouldn't mind throwing a Christiana to the lions. Anyway, you'll have Paul.'

'Fat lot of good he'll be. You know he'll just sit there in silence, staring at them as if they're all mad.'

'He'd be right.'

'Come on. We'll make sure we sit together. We haven't had a good chat in ages.'

'Oh, all right, then.'

'Good woman. Meet you at the front door in fifteen minutes.'

I closed her bedroom door behind me. *Phew!*

I had the distinct feeling that this was going to be a very long night.

There was no need for introductions when we arrived at the restaurant. Unfortunately, we had already met. The two separate camps eyed each other suspiciously: me, Hazel and Paul versus Oisín, Diarmuid, Fionn, Neasa, Iseult and Mona. Sure, we were outnumbered – but we were confident we could take them, being of stronger moral fibre. We nodded to each other as we took our seats. Let the Cold War commence. Christiana didn't know it, but she was Switzerland.

Chris, Hazel and I were the last to arrive. We had been delayed by Chris's last-minute nail-polish crisis: she had been torn between glittery blue and molten violet. Hazel still had a face on her as a result.

And speaking of people having faces on them…. Paul, true to form, had been the first to arrive. This meant that he had spent the last forty minutes enduring a discussion on the latest trends in men's trousers – not the type of thing he normally discussed with his soccer buddies. Judging by the

41

cut of Diarmuid, Oisín and Fionn, brown corduroy flares appeared to be all the rage. As did blue rimless sunglasses worn on the crown of one's head.

'Hey, lads. Going on your holidays?' Hazel said cheerfully as she sat down. She was going for a pre-emptive strike.

The lads looked at one another blankly. Hazel pointed to the top of her head. 'The sunglasses. Or maybe you're expecting a sudden heat wave?'

'Actually, that's the fashion, Hazel,' said Iseult.

'Oh, is it, actually, Iseult? I didn't actually know that. Tell me more.' Hazel poured herself a massive glass of red wine. I sensed danger.

'Has anyone ordered yet?' I said.

'No, we were waiting for you,' answered Paul. Then, under his breath to me, 'Where the hell were you? You wouldn't believe the shite I've just had to listen to.'

'I'm sorry. I couldn't help it. Now please be nice. It's just a few short hours out of your life.'

'That Diarmuid has already taken years off my life. He made a pass at me, you know.'

I tried unsuccessfully not to laugh. Paul, like many red-blooded heterosexual males, had yet to be convinced that all gay men weren't after his body.

'What did you say to him?'

'What could I say? I pretended to misunderstand him.'

I was sorry I'd missed it. 'You must have said something to lead him on, Paul.'

'You're very funny, you know that?'

'Anything in trousers. You just can't be trusted.'

'Stop it.'

'He's a model, you know. I thought it was every man's dream to go out with a model.' Paul didn't find this funny at all. I, on the other hand, was cracking myself up.

'Shut up, Lainey.'

'Slut.'

He didn't dignify that with a response.

After a while he said, 'I suppose those other two are queers as well.'

'Who, Fionn and Oisín? No, they're not gay.'

'Thank God for that. I was beginning to think I was the only straight man here.'

'They're bisexual. So we might both get lucky.'

'I'm going to the jacks.'

'Careful you don't get followed,' I called after him. He glared back at me. Paul was deliciously easy to wind up.

I zoned in on the other conversation that was going on down our end of the table – between Hazel, Iseult and Diarmuid.

'So tell me, Iseult,' said Hazel, far too loudly. 'I'm dying to know. What *is* the new black?'

Iseult eyed Hazel coolly. The fashion editor of an Irish celebrity magazine, she was probably the most copped-on of the group. You could tell that she strongly suspected that she was having the piss taken out of her.

'Well, Hazel, black is always in. But I can see that you're well aware of that. I mean, just look at that *lovely* ensemble you're wearing tonight.'

'This old thing! Shucks, Iseult, I just threw this little number on as I was leaving the flat.'

'You'd never guess.' Iseult's smile rivalled Hazel's for tightness and insincerity.

'Actually, I heard that aubergine was the new black,' said Diarmuid. *For Pete's sake, don't get involved,* I felt like warning him. 'Like Lainey's cardigan.' It wasn't often that I was cast in the role of trendsetter. (I had assumed the cardigan was maroon.)

'Aubergine! Really, Diarmuid?' Hazel trilled. 'Well, what I want to know is, what's the new aubergine?'

'Um….' Poor Diarmuid was stumped.

Just then the food arrived. Saved by the starters. I had ordered deep-fried Brie; I had wanted soup, but I was afraid that somebody might be tempted to use the accompanying bread rolls as ammunition.

Paul came back and sat down.

'What's this supposed to be?' He was staring at his plate in pure disgust.

'I don't know. What did you order?'

'Pork wontons in plum sauce.'

'What's the problem? They look like wontons to me.'

'But there's only four of them!'

Sure enough, four small pork parcels sat forlornly

44

on a large, purple (inedible) lettuce leaf, surrounded by a trickle of brown sauce.

'Hmm. They do look a little bit lonely, all right.'

'Lonely! They're practically in quarantine. I've a good mind to send them back to the kitchen.'

'I wouldn't do that, Paul. The chef will only spit on them and send them back. Here, have some bread.' He had already asked the waitress for a new glass because of an imaginary lipstick-mark. He'd make a great health inspector.

Paul took a slice of fancy bread and bit into it viciously. After a few chews, he screwed up his face.

'What the hell is in this bread?' He inspected it suspiciously. 'It's full of green stuff. They're leaves! Lainey, somebody's put leaves in the bread.'

'They're herbs, Paul. What's wrong with you tonight? You're like a bag of cats.'

His face relaxed, and he took my hand under the table. 'I'm sorry. It's just that I get to spend so little time with you nowadays. The last people I want to share you with are this bunch of tossers.' He squeezed my hand so hard it almost hurt. 'I'm really going to miss you, Lainey.'

I gulped. 'I'll miss you, too.'

He smiled at me, for the first time that night, and kissed me lightly on the cheek. I felt a twinge of something. Regret?

I opted to put it down to indigestion.

Those of us who were having starters finished up. Diarmuid wasn't having a starter because he was on the Atkins diet. Iseult wasn't either, because she was a strict vegan. Neasa wasn't because she was dairy-intolerant, and Mona wasn't because she was following a detox programme.

'Camel!' exclaimed Diarmuid suddenly. I had no idea what he was talking about. The menu was quite unusual, but I hadn't spotted camel on there. Ostrich and shark, perhaps. (*Garçon, je voudrais camel en croute avec petits pois, s'il vous plaît.* One hump or two?)

Everybody looked at Diarmuid, who was red-faced and excited.

'The new aubergine. It's camel.'

'Did I miss something?' whispered Paul.

'Camel. Of course! Thank you so much for enlightening me, Diarmuid. Now I can shop with confidence,' Hazel said gaily. 'More wine, anyone?' Without waiting for a response, she sloshed wine into her own glass, almost up to the rim – a sure sign, as if we needed one, that she was pissed.

Diarmuid looked pleased. Luckily, he was too thick to realise that he was being made a fool of. But Hazel wasn't finished with the poor sod yet.

'Diarmuid, I must tell you what a treat it is to have this opportunity to talk to someone who's so' – she pretended to search for the right phrase – 'in the know. I mean, your hairstyle, for instance; it's so damn *stylish*! Where should someone like, say, Paul go to get a lovely do like that?'

I felt Paul stiffen beside me.

'Oh, do you really like it? Thanks. I got it done in the new hairdresser's in the Powerscourt shopping centre. Hold on, I think I still have the card....' Diarmuid started fishing around in what looked like, but couldn't possibly have been, a handbag.

'Here!' He triumphantly thrust a business card across the table at Paul, who was so dumbstruck, he forgot to say thanks.

'Although, if you ask me,' Diarmuid added, almost coyly, 'your hair is really nice the way it is.'

'I agree,' said Iseult. 'I wouldn't change a thing if I were you.' She gave Paul a predatory smile and a wink. A *wink*!

Are you hitting on my boyfriend, Missus? At least have the good manners to wait till I've gone to the loo or something. I suppose she couldn't contain herself. Paul was probably the only straight man she'd met all month.

I glanced at Paul, to gauge his reaction. He didn't seem to be having any. He was still frozen with embarrassment at Diarmuid's attentions. His cheeks were the new black.

I had been beginning to feel a little sorry for Iseult. Hazel in vicious mode was too hot for most people to handle, even though I knew from past experience that Iseult could bitch for Ireland. But that wink had extinguished my last glimmer of sympathy. *Go get her, Hazel!*

I glanced across at Iseult, who was re-applying her lippy between courses, even though she hadn't

47

actually eaten anything yet. She was peering into a compact mirror, delicately wiping the corners of her mouth with her index finger.

'Oh, yes,' she was saying to Diarmuid, 'scarves *must* be worn long this season. It's absolutely essential.'

Essential for what? World peace? Strangling her with?

She was quite good-looking, I thought grudgingly, if you liked that sort of thing. All cheekbones and snooty expression. Kristin Scott Thomas would be a good choice to play the starring role in the movie of her life.

The main courses arrived. Paul just sat staring at his elf-sized portion of rack of lamb. I thought he might cry. He looked piteously at me. I patted his hand and promised that I'd buy him a bag of chips on the way home.

'Tell me, Lainey,' said Iseult. Warning – bomb alert! 'Where *did* you get that scrumptious cardie?'

'It's not mine. It's Chris's.'

'Ah, I see. That explains it. I thought it wasn't your usual style.'

'My usual style being?' It was a challenge.

Iseult gave a high, tinkly laugh. 'I really couldn't say.'

The wound was stinging but hardly fatal. I maintained a dignified silence. This was because I couldn't think of a suitably bitchy response. I decided to store up the insult for future reference.

Paul and I were the only people at the table having dessert, even though he didn't really like it. He knew the drill: he ordered a dessert, which I helped him pick out, and then I ate at least two-thirds of it. It was a wonderfully guilt-free method of consuming calories. Everyone else ordered their triple skinny lattes or whatever.

As we were finishing up and paying the bill (extortion, according to an outraged Paul), Chris skipped excitedly over to our side of the table. At least someone was enjoying herself.

'Hey, guys, let's all go to Manilow's!'

'God, no, Chris! Manilow's is so two weeks ago. Let's go to Mango's,' said Iseult.

I had been to Manilow's the week before, and it had seemed fine to me. I decided I'd better not admit to this for fear of being branded a social pariah.

'Are you coming, Lainey?' asked Chris.

I was about to agree until Paul shot me an urgent, pleading look.

'Um, maybe I should take Hazel home. She's a little the worse for wear.'

This was no lie. Hazel was slumped over the table, singing gently to herself.

'Are you coming out dancing with us, Hazel?' Chris shouted in her ear.

Hazel slid up and looked blearily at us from beneath her mussed-up hair. She slurred aggressively, 'I'm not going out anywhere with that bunch of wan–'

'Okay, Hazel, let's be having you.' Not allowing her to finish the sentence – although I think we all got the general gist – Paul hauled Hazel up by the elbow, simultaneously prising the wine glass from her hand and masterfully ignoring her squeaks of protest.

I turned to Chris and hugged her apologetically. 'You can see she really needs to be brought home to bed. Paul and I will look after her. You go out and enjoy yourself, and I'll see you in the morning.'

Except that I didn't see her the next morning, because she spent the night with one of the bi-sexuals. Come to think of it, I never found out which one.

Chapter Four

My first glimpse of Ballyknock was from the back of a J.J. Kavanagh bus. I was pleasantly surprised. It was a beautiful day. We were experiencing the type of Indian summer we often get in this country as compensation for the lack of an actual summer: a blazing hot day in September, when all the kids are back at school, sitting in sweltering hot class-rooms, gazing longingly out of the windows. Even now, this time of year made me want to run out and buy a new geometry set. I was reminded of knees skinned on hot tarmac playgrounds. It was a time of new terms and new starts, almost like a second New Year – a second chance to make reso-lutions that you might actually stick to. My current

New Year's resolutions had been long forgotten. I vaguely recalled something about losing a stone in weight and breaking it off with Paul.

The bus crawled along Main Street. I remember thinking that every piss-ant little town in Ireland must have a Main Street, consisting of a church, a chipper, a newsagent-cum-family-supermarket and a boutique selling half-slips and triple packs of granny knickers. Oh, and six pubs. Ballyknock was no exception. Then there was the solicitor's office, of course. The bus moved slowly enough for me to have a good look at the new premises. Not bad. Could do with a lick of paint. And then the bus swung over the bridge.

I literally gasped with delight. The old medieval bridge, reinforced with ugly concrete and steel over time to accommodate the passing trucks, straddled a wide blue expanse of river, bordered on either side by grassy green banks. Old mill-houses, some discarded, some still in use, lined the riverbanks at intervals. The scene was completed by a pair of swans, floating regally by as if posing for a portrait. I could get used to this.

The bus stopped outside Power's pub. Power's Undertakers were next door. Padraig Power Auctioneers were across the street. Obviously Tyrone's family were the Kennedys of Ballyknock. I thanked the driver as I got off the bus, heaving my bulging rucksack behind me. He seemed to know every passenger personally, except for me, and they all knew him by name: Thanks, Jimmy; see you next week, please God. I went into Power's (the pub, not the undertaker's), as per my instructions from Tyrone, to order a cab.

The bar was almost empty. There was a middle-aged man behind the counter, polishing a pint glass with an ancient-looking tea-towel. Two old lads, wearing matching cloth caps, perched on barstools opposite him. As I entered, they all stopped mid-sentence and stared at me. I thought for one terrible moment that this was one of those country pubs I'd heard of where they didn't serve women. Get back to that kitchen sink where you belong, Missus.

'Hello. I'm Elena Malone.'

More blank stares.

'Tyrone Power sent me.'

The transformation was spontaneous.

'Ah, you're Tyrone's girl. Come in and let's be having a look at you.'

I advanced slowly and uncertainly, embarrassed by the scrutiny. I felt like I was ten years old again, being inspected by elderly grand-uncles at some gruesome family function.

'Will you have a drink, love? Tom here is buying.'

'No, thanks. I'm just looking for a taxi. I have to get to …' I fished a screwed-up Post-it out of my pocket. 'Ard-ske-ha.' I pronounced the name awkwardly.

'Go 'way out of that. Sure I'll drive you there meself.'

53

'Do you know where it is, then?'

The three men laughed like drains. The older of the two customers – who, I later found out, was aptly known as Tom Delaney of the Rusty Teeth – erupted into an alarming fit of coughing. His companion – who went by the name of Shem – gave him a thump on the back, and he stopped coughing and re-lit his pipe. Mellow Virginia. Reminded me of my granddad.

'You could say that, love. Didn't I grow up there?' He wiped his right hand on the tea-towel and extended it. 'I'm John Power, Tyrone's brother.'

I shook his hand. 'Pleasure to meet you, Mr Power.'

'You may as well call me Johnny. Everybody else does. Besides, every second man in town is Mr Power. You'll cause terrible confusion.'

More guttural guffaws all round.

'Will you have a pint of stout, love?' This was from Tom of the Rusty Teeth, who I could have sworn winked at me, although it might just have been a twitch.

'What are you thinking of, man?' demanded Shem. 'Sure you know these young ones from Dublin drink nothing but those Bacardi Breezers. Terrible stuff. Tastes like donkey's piss. Isn't that right, love?'

'Actually, a glass of Guinness would be lovely.'

The glass of stout was placed ceremoniously before me. I picked it up and, even with my low standards of hygiene, was slightly disgusted at the way the bottom of the glass stuck to the counter. I drank deeply and gratefully, savouring the bitterness and carefully licking the line of white foam off my top lip.

I surveyed my surroundings. The pub also served as a general grocer's. Side by side with the many bottles behind the bar were packets of cornflakes, shoe polish in black and neutral, and pink butterfly slides for little girls' hair. I noticed with childish delight the three big jars of bonbons: toffee, lemon and original. I was going to have to get me some of those. But not today. I was the new solicitor in town; I had my reputation to consider. I'd have to send some little kid in to get them for me on the sly. On the wall beside me was an old black-and-white photo of a group of moustachioed men wearing old-fashioned three-piece suits and funny hats. They were standing outside a slightly – but not very – different-looking Power's pub. Previous generations of Powers, I guessed; one of the men looked spookily like Tyrone. This place was the real thing, all right. I had been in many a fake olde original pub in Dublin; this was the ambience that they had been trying to create.

A settled-looking woman, a pinny tied tightly across her ample hips, had materialised behind the bar. She was sporting a suspiciously dark head of hair for her age. She hummed to herself, swishing a bright-blue feather duster delicately along the bar, and looked at me quizzically from time to time, a half-smile on her face. I could tell she was dying to find out who I was. Finally, unable to contain herself any longer, she nudged the barman.

'Are you not going to introduce me, Johnny?'

'Elaine, this is the wife, Bridie Power. Bridie, this is Elaine, Tyrone's new girl.'

'Actually, it's Elena. But you can call me Lainey. Pleased to meet you.'

'The new solicitor, is it? Well, I never would have guessed. You don't look one bit like a solicitor – does she, Johnny? God bless us, you're very young. And you're going to be living up on top of that hill in Ardskeha all on your own?'

'Well, I am, yes.' I was from the city, for God's sake, land of joyriders, muggers and drive-by shootings; I could surely handle a few months alone in a country cottage.

'God bless us and save us – a lovely young girl like you…. Are you not married?'

'No.'

Shem made a sound that I guessed passed for a suggestive laugh in these parts. 'We won't have much trouble setting up a laying hen like you.'

'A what?'

'A laying hen. A young girl with good earning potential, like a teacher or a nurse. A solicitor, now – that's like landing the goose with the golden egg.' The three men shook with laughter and Tom had another coughing fit.

'I already have a boyfriend, thank you.' I could

feel myself getting ready to mount my high horse.

'Does he hurl?' asked Shem.

'No. He plays soccer, though.'

I might as well have told them that he was a dab hand at needlepoint, judging by the hilarity it caused.

'Don't you be minding those oul' fellas, Elaine, love. What do they know? I'm sure your boyfriend is a fine lad. But, just in case things don't work out with him, I have seven lovely lads of my own – three of them not married, even though they're getting on a bit now. I'm sure one of them would do nicely for you.'

I had a flashback of *Seven Brides for Seven Brothers*. When the brothers decide they need wives, they all go into town, kidnap the women of their choice and carry them kicking and screaming back to the homestead.

'Anyway,' Bridie continued, 'we're keeping you too long. I'm sure you must be keen to settle into your new place. I'll take over here, Johnny. You give Elaine a lift up to Ardskeha. Just wait till I give her a few bits to help her settle in.' Bridie disappeared mysteriously through a door at the back of the bar, and emerged a couple of minutes later laden down by a bulging paper bag.

'Now' – she plonked it down on the counter – 'I've put in a carton of eggs, freshly laid this morning by our own hens – what you in the city call free-range. And there's a soda bread I baked

57

this morning – there's only a few slices gone out of it. And there's a pot of strawberry jam for you, love.'

'You'll enjoy that,' said Johnny. 'Bridie's strawberry jam won first prize at the Mivik show the other week.'

'It was the same batch, too.' Bridie smiled proudly. 'Although I suppose you'll be making your own jam soon enough. There's plenty of blackberries up around Ardskeha way, and you'll have your own crab-apple trees in the garden. They make a lovely jelly.'

I smiled politely. Why on earth would anyone bother making jam when they could buy a perfectly good pot of it in the supermarket?

'And I've put in a few teabags and a carton of milk, so as you can make yourself a nice cup of tea in your new place.'

'Thank you. How much do I owe you?'

Bridie held up her hand. 'Don't be insulting me, now, girl. Think of it as a gift to welcome you to Ballyknock. I hope you'll be very happy here.'

I thanked her profusely and followed Johnny out of the pub door. She called out to me as I left, 'Don't be a stranger, now. You know where we are if you need anything.'

I had trouble keeping up with Johnny. He moved surprisingly quickly for a man of his age; I estimated that he was about sixty, but he was lithe and wiry and seemed full of nervous energy. He

58

had lifted the stuffed bag and the rucksack out of my arms as if they were dead leaves. He stopped beside a Peugeot 405 diesel with a 90 KK reg; it was parked high up on the narrow pavement, seemingly oblivious to the double yellow lines. It was danger-red, and the seat-covers were leopard-skin. He opened the passenger door for me with a great flourish, as if I were a movie star and he were my chauffeur helping me into my limousine. I stepped in, over a jumble of receipts, fag packets, Mars bar wrappers and a disembodied doll's head. There was a faint whiff of something that I was later able to identify as slurry.

Without a discernible glance into his mirrors, Johnny took off at high speed. The engine sounded like a lawnmower. Without indicating or slowing down, he took the first left turn we came to. I double-checked that my seat-belt was properly fastened. The car crawled up a steep hill and the engine roared painfully, as if the machine was about to take off like some old-fashioned, dilapidated fighter plane. I hoped there was a life-jacket under my seat. Can someone please pass the sick-bag?

After we had hurtled along for a while without crashing, I decided to chance opening one eye. I found that we were speeding down a narrow, tree-lined avenue. I looked to my left and realised how far up into the hills we had already climbed. Through the trees, I could see the edge of the village nestling in the valley. The river wound about the houses like a long blue ribbon. Ahead, the trees seemed to stretch into infinity. They reached out to one another across the road, forming a verdant arch; sunlight dappled through at intervals, making the leaves sparkle like so many emeralds. This wasn't half bad. It sure beat the soggy sheep and grey rocks of County Galway.

As we climbed higher and higher, the trees gave way to rolling green hills that undulated softly into the distance. We passed a field of black-and-white cows, like the scattered pieces of a jigsaw puzzle. A field of cloud-like sheep, with black faces and ears like handlebars. A field of horses in varying shades of chestnut and grey. At one point, a rabbit scuttled across the road in front of us, narrowly avoiding the bald tyres of the Peugeot. I imagined that Johnny Power was a prime suspect in a large percentage of the roadkill incidents in Ballyknock and its environs.

The man himself cleared his throat and turned to me. He yelled something that I couldn't quite make out over the roar of the engine.

'Say that again, Johnny.'

'I said, why don't you have a car?'

'I do. It's in being serviced.' I didn't like the way he kept turning to look at me every time he spoke. *Keep your eyes on the road, for God's sake, man.*

'What do you drive?'

'An Audi TT convertible.'

'Begod,' he cackled, 'Tyrone must be paying you too much.'

'You can never be paid too much,' I yelled back.

'You might be right there, love.'

'Watch out for the tractor!' I screeched as a blue tractor loomed up around the bend, directly ahead of us. The Peugeot emitted an almighty screech and skidded to a halt, just inches away from the massive back tyre of the tractor.

'Jaysus, that was a close one. The brakes are working, anyways,' said Johnny cheerfully.

I, a Catholic of the very definitely non-practising variety, uttered a silent prayer of thanksgiving.

I twisted around in my seat and peeped out through the bars of my fingers. The tractor was a 1970 reg. It was even older than me, for God's sake; no wonder it was such a wreck. My eyes travelled upwards to the cab, which was open at the back. It was a convertible! Not pleasant driving in inclement weather, I guessed; but on a fine September evening such as this, when it was hot enough for a man to drive along without a shirt on his back, I could think of no better mode of transport. Yes, I thought, as I lowered my hands from my eyes and feasted them on the broad, tanned expanse of muscle and sinew before me, I heartily approved. I watched, spellbound, as the owner of the back braked the tractor, his muscles rippling enticingly.

Johnny stuck his head out of the car window and shouted, 'Well, boy, how are you going?'

'Ah, is it yourself, Da? I'm grand.' And, with that, the godlike creature hopped out onto the roadway.

Maybe we had crashed after all. I was really dead, and this was an angel come to carry me away. I fervently wished that I had time to brush my hair.

'What do we have here?' His voice matched his torso, strong and powerful. He had ducked his head and was looking in at me through the driver's window, grinning his head off. Yes: very soft on the eye indeed.

'This is Tyrone's girl, Elaine ... what did you say your last name was, again?'

'Malone. You can call me Lainey.' I extended my hand eagerly past Johnny's face, nearly whacking the poor man in the nose. 'Pleased to meet you.'

'And I'm very pleased to meet you too, Lainey. I'm Jack Power, Johnny and Bridie's favourite son.' He wiped his right hand on the leg of his overalls, which had probably once been navy blue and which made his hand even dirtier. I didn't care. He engulfed my hand in his. It was the size of a shovel.

'Would you go 'way out of that. There are no favourites in the Power household. Did you move that heifer today?'

'I did.'

'How was she looking?'

'Could've been better. I think we should get Matt to have a look at her.'

Johnny turned to me. 'Matt's another of my sons. He's a vet.'

There was another one like Jack back at the ranch! In fact, hadn't Bridie said she had seven sons?

My sense of optimism about the whole Ballyknock experiment reached a new high.

'Anyway, we'd better be off. I've to take this young lady up to Power's Cottage.'

'Is that where you're staying, Lainey?'

I nodded.

'On your own?'

'All on my own.'

'We'll have to make sure you don't feel too lonely.'

I nodded again and grinned foolishly. I hoped that meant what I thought it meant. Jack winked at me, then stood up and banged the roof of the car twice in farewell. It felt like his hand was going to come right through the rusty exterior.

We headed off again at breakneck speed. I almost felt sorry for the car; it had to put up with a lot. I closed my eyes again and braced myself for the next near miss. My foot reached for the imaginary brake half a dozen times. Every now and then I opened my eyes to try and admire the scenery. It really was stunning. Not a bad place to die, I reflected.

One thing was worrying me, though. We seemed to be driving for miles and miles, deeper and deeper into the wilderness. I hadn't noticed many houses, either. I wanted badly to ask, 'Are we there yet?' but I didn't want to risk sounding like a pathetic child.

I needn't have worried. Without warning, to me or any other drivers who happened to have the misfortune of sharing the road, Johnny made a sharp right turn into what could only be described as a boreen. This was the steepest hill we'd been on yet. The trusty Peugeot laboured up the windy road, roaring like some injured wild animal. I thought I could feel my ears popping, but surely that was just my imagination. I wouldn't have to worry about the house flooding, that was for sure.

Without bothering to change gear – sure, why would you want to be bothering with any of that oul' malarkey anyway? – Johnny brought the car, skidding and complaining, to an abrupt halt.

'Here we are. Home sweet home.'

Thank you, God! I exited the car as if it were on fire, delighted just to be alive. I felt like kissing the earth, like the Pope does when he visits a new country. And a new country it was.

Chapter Five

I was delighted to discover that my home for the coming months was a city girl's dream of the charming country cottage. Two hundred years old, but recently refurbished; oodles of character, but with all mod cons.

The cottage had been donated to the Power family by an extremely generous neighbour at the time of the Famine, when the Powers had been evicted from their former home by the archetypal evil landlord. Johnny delivered this brief potted history of the house as he carried in my bags. He made sure I was settled in before he tore back down the hill in his red chariot, no doubt causing small furry animals to run for their lives. I waved him off until the car was a red dot on the horizon, and then went back inside.

I felt very happy – even though the place was tiny. It was hard to believe that the cottage had once accommodated a family of eleven. I would barely be able to fit myself in, with all my clothes and useless knick-knacks – even though I'd planned to leave half my stuff in Dublin. But I had a good feeling about this place. *A person could be very happy here,* I thought.

I was still wrapped up in warm, positive feelings as I snuggled up in my bed that night. I had just passed a pleasant evening curled up on a very comfortable, chocolate-brown, distressed-leather two-seater in front of the modest fire that I'd lit. Some thoughtful person – I guessed that a member of the Power clan was the kind culprit – had provided a wicker basket full of briquettes, logs and firelighters.

Above the fireplace was an old framed photograph of a stern, handsome woman in old-fashioned dress. It had been taken in the days before people said 'cheese' for the camera. Her eyes had a disconcerting habit of following me around the room. It was a little creepy, to tell the truth. I'd have to find out who she was.

I had feasted on a tea of scrambled eggs – just like Mother used to make – and, for dessert, the best soda bread and strawberry jam that money couldn't buy. This was all washed down with copious mugs of steaming hot tea, accompanied by two Marlboro

Lights and the latest Stephen King. I sighed as I puffed away. This was nice. No Paul to complain.

I was blown away by the absolute silence of the place. Our flat in Dublin backed onto a major thoroughfare, and I had grown up living in the 'burbs; the lack of noise pollution – traffic, sirens, car alarms, raucous shouts from fights outside the local kippy chippy – was quite daunting. Not that I missed these sounds, any more than I missed having to listen to Hazel row on the phone with her parents, or Christiana having sex with her latest acquisition, through the paper-thin apartment walls. I supposed I'd get used to it, this weird blanket of silence.

And there was something else, too: the darkness. I had forgotten what country dark was like – that rich, deep, secret darkness that results from a total absence of street lighting. I opened the front door at one stage, captivated by the spectacle of a multitude of diamanté stars piercing the big, black, velvet sky. I stood on the two-hundred-year-old doorstep, thinking of that song, 'The Night Has a Thousand Eyes'. And then I gave myself the creeps. An unknown animal hollered into the darkness and I hurried back inside and closed the door on the night, before it could suck me in – envelop me. Maybe I should lay off the Stephen King novels for a while.

But anyway, there I was, lying snuggled up underneath my big eiderdown quilt, revelling in the feel of the crisp, clean cotton sheets. (The all-seeing mother-eye had forced me to wash up before

I retired.) The phone was beside the bed, just a hand-stretch away, and so was the bedside lamp. I had put a chair up against the inside of the bedroom door – just to make myself feel more secure, you understand. Oh, and I had placed a kitchen knife under the mattress. I laughed at my own stupidity, telling myself that it was just for the first few nights, until I got used to the alien surroundings. To the darkness. To the silence. I eventually drifted off to sleep, counting, not sheep, but the hairs on Jack Power's chest.

I woke with a start and looked around wildly. Where the fuck was I?

Realisation dawned, and I checked the time. I had been asleep for about two hours. What had woken me? I tried to remember if I'd been having some kind of strange dream. Definitely no more horror books for me; from now on I was going on a strict diet of chick-lit and the autobiographies of former Spice Girls.

What the hell … In one swift movement I leapt out of bed and flicked the switch on the bedside lamp, managing to knock it over in the process. I fumbled around for the knife under the mattress. There it was again – the noise! I stood in the middle of the bedroom floor, looking from left to right with terrified eyes, holding the knife aloft, legs planted wide apart as if I was ready to take flight or spring upon somebody. I must have looked like a bad scene from *Xena Warrior Princess*. The episode where Xena swaps her leather tunic for Marks & Sparks teddy-bear pyjamas.

I jumped again as the noise was repeated. The roof – it was coming from the roof! I looked up, terrified, at the Velux window, half-expecting to see a man's face grinning maniacally in at me. There was nobody there.

There it was again. It was a very definite scratching sound – furtive…. And again! But this time it wasn't a scratching. More like a creaking. Rhythmic. Repetitive. More like … footsteps. And it wasn't coming from the roof, I realised with a sick, heavy feeling in my stomach. It was coming from the attic.

For the second time that day and in about five years, I prayed, with sincerity and from the bottom of my heart. With a further sinking feeling, I noticed that the attic trapdoor was in the bedroom ceiling. Why hadn't I listened to my father? He had been right all along. Lone females getting murdered to death in isolated country cottages – you heard about it all the time….

'Who's there?' I asked ludicrously. My voice came out in a strangled whisper. I cleared my throat. 'Who's there?' I croaked loudly. Of course they were going to answer. *Hi, it's me. Billy the axe murderer. I've come to hack you into a million pieces. I hope tonight is convenient for you.*

'I'm calling the gardaí!' I shouted. Even I detected the dangerous note of hysteria in my voice. This time it had an effect. The footsteps broke into a run.

Omigod!

I dived on the phone and jabbed 999, barely registering that my fingers were trembling. At least the phone was working. I had half-expected it to be cut off, just like in the old horror movies.

'Hello, what service do you require?'

'Police! Quickly! There's someone trying to break in! I'm on my own!' I gibbered.

'Calm down, please. Give me your name and address.'

I did, suppressing the urge to scream at the woman. How could she be so calm? Did she not know that this was an emergency? (Presumably she did, seeing as it was her job to man the emergency phone line, and all.) As soon as she had assured me that somebody was on the way, I hung up and shouted up at the attic defiantly: 'Now, you scumbag, I've called the police and they'll be here any minute! And,' I added, as an afterthought, 'I'll have you know that I'm a solicitor!' That should do the trick, all right. What was I going to do? Send him a summons by registered post? Buy him a house?

While I waited for the gardaí to arrive, I sat like a statue at the edge of the bed, knife in my right hand, phone beside my left. I stared at the attic trapdoor for the entire time, afraid to take my eyes off it for even a second in case a murderous lunatic burst through.

At first I thought he had gone. Everything was quiet for a long time. How had he got out? How had he got *in*? I would have to get the gardaí to investigate.… But every now and then I would hear a furtive creak. He was still there, all right. Why hadn't he tried to escape? Why hadn't he attacked? And where were the gardaí? They were taking their time. It would never take this long in Dublin. Mind you, I would never have found myself in this position in Dublin, because I was never on my own at night. I was going straight back home. I would ring Tyrone first thing in the morning – if I made it through the night, that was – and tell him I couldn't do it. He'd understand when he heard what a terrifying ordeal I'd been through. Where were the bloody gardaí?

At last, I heard the sound of a car coming at considerable speed up the hill. Thanks be to God! The light of the headlights filled the bedroom and broke me out of my trance. Relief flooding my system, I jumped up from the bed and flew to the bedroom door, pulling the chair out of the way. I ran out to the front door and went weak with joy at the sight of two burly uniformed gardaí.

'Oh, thank God, you came.' I grabbed the policeman nearest to me by the arm and dragged him into the bedroom.

'You're all right, Miss. You're safe now. Did you scare him off when you woke up?'

'No, he's still here,' I hissed urgently. 'Up in the attic.' I pointed up at the attic door.

The two gardaí stood in my bedroom and looked up at the tiny trapdoor in the ceiling.

'Do you have a ladder handy?' asked the second garda.

'I don't know. There might be one in the shed.'

'I'll go check.' Garda Number Two started to leave the room. Just then, a scuffling sound came from the attic again, loud and clear. It was as if someone was crawling along on his hands and knees. I gripped Garda Number One's arm again.

'There it is again! He's still up there. We've got him trapped.' I smiled triumphantly, feeling like Nancy Drew after solving some particularly trouble-some mystery.

The two gardaí exchanged a look. I couldn't interpret their expressions.

'Is that the noise you heard before, Miss?'

'Yes! Quick, get the ladder.' I was crazily glad that he'd called me 'Miss' instead of 'Madam'.

Garda Number One nodded at Garda Number Two, who went out. We could hear him rummag-ing around in the shed. Every now and then, a loud scuffling noise came from up above. I clung to Number One's uniformed arm harder each time, forgetting all about being proper. The garda glanced at me uncertainly. Looking back, I think he might have been a little embarrassed.

At last Number Two came back in, bearing a rusty, paint-splattered ladder. He ascended jauntily and began pushing at the attic door in a manner that I could only describe as careless.

'Watch out – he may be armed!' I hissed urgently.

The garda peered down at me, a bemused (or was it amused?) expression on his face. For the first time in my life, I wished fervently that Ireland had an armed police force. Then they could blow the bastard's head off and plead self-defence. It would serve him right for frightening the shite out of me.

I dug my fingers deeper into Number One's arm and shrank against him. I wanted to run out of the room, but my feet seemed rooted to their spot on the bedroom carpet. It occurred to me that the gardaí should have made sure that I was safely out of the vicinity. Surely this was negligent of them.

The upper half of Number Two's body disappeared into the attic. We could see the beam of his torch sweeping back and forth; then he swung his legs up, and we could hear him walking slowly around. He seemed to be up there for an age. *What's going on?* I felt like yelling up at him. The garda beside me seemed very relaxed. I would have thought he'd be getting ready to attack, in case Number Two needed backup.

I couldn't help uttering a short scream as a head appeared in the trapdoor. Number Two was peering down at us with something like a smirk playing about his lips.

'Well?' said Number One. Number Two nodded at him and then looked at me.

'I'm afraid you've got rats.'

This time I really screamed.

Chapter Six

The alarm drilled into my eardrums at 7.30 a.m. I jerked out of a fitful sleep and, for the second time that morning, wondered where the hell I was. After a few seconds, I recognised the blurry lines of my new bedroom, pressed the snooze button and lay back in the bed and stretched.

And then I remembered. I groaned loudly, but there was no one to hear. No one to tell me that last night had been only a nightmare. But, even if I hadn't been on my own, nobody could have performed that particular miracle for me.

After the two laughing policemen had left, I had lain awake for most of the night, ears strained for that evil scuffling. At one point, just as I was at last managing to drop off, a strand of my hair had fallen across my face and I had leapt up, shouting hysterically, convinced that a rat had just brushed past me. Sleep hadn't visited again until about half an hour before the alarm had gone off. It wasn't exactly what I would call wonderful preparation for the first day in my new office.

Rather than lie there and think of my new furry flatmates, not to mention my humiliation at having called the gardaí out to investigate the 'intruder' (I groaned again), I decided to get up. I checked my slippers carefully for signs of life and tiptoed cautiously into the bathroom. There was no way I was staying in this rat-infested dump. I was going to ring Tyrone at nine on the dot, and he could damn well arrange alternative accommodation.

I arrived outside my new office in the village of Ballyknock at five to nine precisely. I had been subjected to the hackney driver's incessant questioning for the previous ten minutes, and my foul humour had worsened. What I wouldn't have done for an O'Brien's double espresso.... I was supposed to be meeting my new secretary – with my new key – at nine. I had decided to arrive a few minutes early, just to show that I was on the ball.

At 9.15 I was still standing there. This had gone beyond a joke. I was beginning to get curious looks from passers-by. Several cars even slowed down to get a better look at me – we're not talking kerb-crawling here, just pure nosiness. I barely restrained myself from making rude hand gestures. Hardly the impression one would like to convey on one's first day in a new town in one's capacity as a solicitor.

'There you are, dear. Have you been waiting long?' A plumpish woman with rosy cheeks and short blonde hair bustled down the street towards me. She was clearly out of breath and struggling to carry several bulky plastic bags. I judged her to be in her early forties. Forty-five would hold her.

'Only half an hour,' I lied.

'Oh, you poor love. Let's go inside and get ourselves a nice cup of coffee.' She dropped a couple of her bags and held out her hand. 'I'm Patricia. I hope you're Lainey – otherwise I'm after making an awful eejit of myself.'

I took her hand, shook it in a dazed fashion and confirmed that I was indeed Lainey Malone.

'Well, Lainey, you are a pretty girl, aren't you?'

I smiled uncertainly and blushed a little. It was very nice to be called a pretty girl, but surely that wasn't the usual way to greet your new boss.

Patricia fumbled in an oversized handbag and pulled out a massive set of keys. She tried about ten of them in the lock before happening upon the right one. She kept talking the entire time.

'You'll never guess what happened to me this morning.'

I shook my head: no, I'd never guess.

'I was getting the kids ready for school, and didn't I have them all dressed and ready to go out the door, and didn't Mikey only go and spill his entire bowl of Coco Pops all the way down his clean shirt, and didn't I have to iron another one for him and wasn't I fit to hit him, and of course then we were stuck in the traffic on Main Street and I was late, and there's you, poor love, standing out on your own in the cold on your very first day in Ballyknock looking like nobody's child, but they are giving it good for next week, mind....' And on she went. I felt fit to hit little Mikey myself.

At last she found the correct key, and I entered what was to be my work-home for the next nine months. If I had thought the cottage was small....

The new premises of Tyrone Power & Co. consisted of an office for me (I could have cried, comparing it to my beautiful office back in Dublin) and an office-cum-reception-area for Patricia. This latter area housed a photocopier, a fax machine and that most essential piece of office equipment – a kettle. I watched gratefully as Patricia started fiddling around with it. My gratitude turned to consternation as she removed a large bottle of still mineral water from one of her bags and proceeded to fill the kettle with the contents.

'Is there no sink?'

'God, no, dear. Sure, how could you get a sink into this place? It's far too small.'

Silly me.

'Is there a toilet, even?'

'Not at all!' She thought this was very funny.

'Well, what do we … do?'

'The bookies upstairs have said we can use their loo.'

How kind.

Maybe I could arrange a transfer to the London office instead.

Patricia redeemed herself by making me the most righteous cup of coffee. I holed myself up in my office for the next hour and tried to organise myself. This entailed ringing and e-mailing all my friends and family members to give them my new details. Well, what if they needed to contact me urgently?

After a while, Patricia stuck her head around the door (without knocking, of course. What would have been the point, anyway? The walls were paper-thin and we could hear every word the other said).

'How are you getting on?'

'Fine. And the coffee was lovely; thank you.'

'You're more than welcome, my dear. Tomorrow I'll bring in some scones. How's everything up at Power's Cottage?'

'Not great. I have a bad case of rats. I'll have to find somewhere else to stay.'

'Rats! God love you! I'll get on to the brother-in-law right away. He's into the pest control.' She made it sound as if hunting down vermin was his hobby. 'He'll have you sorted today. There'll be no need for you to move out for even one night.'

'Thanks, Patricia – that really would be terrific.'

'I'll go ring him. Then I'm off to do my grocery shopping.'

'What – now?' I glanced at the clock. It was ten to eleven.

'Well, yes. I always do my weekly shop on a Monday morning. The supermarket is nice and empty then.' Her face was full of innocent surprise. Imagine me not knowing that she always did her grocery shopping on a Monday morning.

As soon as Patricia left the building, I rang Tyrone. I was put through to Miss Moneypenny.

'Oh, hi, Barb. Can I speak to Tyrone, please?'

'Is it important? He is very busy this morning, you know.'

'Yes, it's important,' I snapped. *Cow.*

'Lainey! How goes it?' boomed Tyrone.

'Well, let's see. The house you kindly lent me is crawling with rats, you couldn't swing a kitten in the office, let alone go to the toilet, and my new secretary – who thinks I'm a pretty little thing, by the way – is off doing her grocery shopping.'

Tyrone hooted with laughter. 'So far, so good, then.'

'Whatever.'

'Never mind. You've just got off to a bad start. The office is only temporary, you know that; as soon as something better comes on the market we'll snap it up. Get Patricia onto the rat problem. Her brother-in-law –'

79

'I know. She already told me,' I said tersely.

'Fair enough. What do you make of her?'

'She's very nice, Tyrone, but … I don't know. Do you really think she's suitable?'

'She may seem a little unorthodox, but just you wait and see. She types up a storm, and her local knowledge is second to none.'

'You mean she's a gossip.'

'Don't knock it. You'll discover that kind of thing is very useful in the country. You're just a Dublin snob, that's your problem.'

'I beg your –'

'Ah, get over yourself, girl. I'm only pulling your leg.'

We shot the breeze, both business and personal, for another ten minutes or so; then Tyrone had to go because Barb had buzzed him a total of four times. I was willing to lay bets that it wasn't about anything important. It was fortunate for her that she managed to keep her jealousy reined in when it came to female clients; otherwise he would have had no choice but to fire her, damn good secretary or no.

My first morning on the job whizzed by. At a few minutes to one, I stuck my head into Patricia's office.

'What way will we work lunch? Do you want to go now for an hour and I'll go when you come back, or what?'(Even though she'd only been back from her shopping expedition for forty-five minutes.)

'There's no need for that. I'll just lock up and we can both go.'

'But what if somebody rings when we're both out?'

'Sure, that's what God invented answering machines for, girl. Besides, who'd be ringing anyway? All the solicitors' offices in the county close for lunch; and if it's a client and if it's that important, they can always ring back at two.'

This did have a peculiar type of logic to it.

'Right, so.' I shrugged. 'You'd better show me how to work the alarm.'

Patricia duly showed me how to activate and de-activate it, and I made a mental note of the code. As we were both leaving, she whispered confidentially to me, 'Don't worry if you forget the code and set it off accidentally. It's not connected up to the Garda station anyhow.'

You what?

'We thought about connecting it, but it'd be too much trouble. The likes of the wind or kids messing around would be setting it off all the time, and we'd keep getting calls at all hours of the night.'

'But what if somebody breaks in?'

'Sure, there's nothing to take.'

'Not yet. But soon we're going to have confidential files.'

'If any of the eejits around here broke in, they wouldn't know what to take. They might run off with the kettle, but that would be about it.'

'Even so, I'm not happy about that. I'm going to call Tyrone about it this afternoon.'

'You do that, love, if it makes you feel better,' said Patricia, patting me on the cheek and smiling kindly at me. (No, you didn't read that wrong: my secretary patted me – *me*, her boss – on the cheek.)

It was most definitely time for lunch.

I let myself back in at five to two. There was no sign of Patricia, but that was okay. There was no sign of her at 2.30 either. That wasn't okay. At 2.32 she breezed in through the front door and beamed at me.

'Ah, hello. Did you have a nice lunch, dear?'

'What time do you call this?' I faced her, arms folded tightly across my chest, brows knitted into what I hoped was a stern frown.

She frowned back at me. 'Is your clock not working? Don't worry, I'll have a look at it. It probably just needs new batteries.'

I looked at her face and realised that she was totally sincere.

And that was the last time I tried to be the big Boss Woman.

At about 3.30 that afternoon, from behind my closed office door, I heard the front door opening and Patricia's loud and cheerful greeting.

'Ah, is it yourself, Murt! How are you keeping?'

'Ah, you know, Patricia – draggin' the devil. Yourself?' It was an old man's voice.

'I'm grand, Murt. What can I do for you on this fine day?'

'I want to see the solicitor.'

'Hold on now, and I'll see what I can do.' She stuck her head around my office door for the tenth time that afternoon. This time she looked particularly excited.

'You've got your first client.'

'Has he got an appointment?'

Patricia was clearly taken aback. 'Well, no, he hasn't. But I thought that, since it's your first day and you're not that busy yet, you might be able to squeeze him in.'

'Who is he?'

'Murt O'Brien. His people come from Dunmore way, his mother was a Brennan from Oldtown and his father ran the local hardware store. He married one of the O'Byrne girls out of the factory and his daughter is married to Tommy Hennessy, my second cousin once removed on my mother's side – they're after building a gorgeous extension –'

'All right. Show him in,' I said, clearing a space on my desk. 'Only tell him he'll have to make an appointment next time.'

I felt quite excited, really. My first Ballyknock client!

An extremely old man wearing a shiny black suit and a fedora hat entered the room. His face looked

83

as if it was made of old brown leather. He stopped short of my desk and executed what I guessed was his version of a double take.

'Who are you?'

I flashed him a professional smile and extended my right hand. 'Lainey Malone. Pleased to meet you.'

He didn't take it. 'Where's Tyrone Power?'

'Mr Power is going to be in Dublin for the next few months. I'm afraid you'll have to make do with me for the time being.'

'I want to see Tyrone.'

'I believe there's a train leaving for Dublin at six.'

The old man stared at me long and hard. Then something flickered behind his eyes and he sat down across from me.

'I want to buy some land.'

'Well, you've come to the right place. I'll just take your details first. Name?'

'Murt O'Brien.'

'Murt. That's unusual. Is it short for Murtagh?'

He gave me a funny look. 'You're not from around here, are you?'

'No, I'm from Dublin.'

'That would explain a lot. Murt is short for Michael.'

'Address?' I wasn't really warming to him.

'Chapel Lane, Ballyknock.'

'And that's in County Kilkenny....' I confirmed, writing it down.

'No. Outer Mongolia.' I looked up at him sharply. The ghost of what was probably a smile played about his shrunken lips.

'Does your house on Chapel Lane have a number?'

'What would I be needing a number for? Haven't I lived there all me life? Everybody knows me.'

Yes, and I'm sure everybody loves you, too, you grumpy old git. 'Now, PPS number, please.'

'What do you need that for?' he snapped.

'The Revenue has to be informed of every property transaction in the State.'

'I don't want that shower knowing my business.'

'I'm afraid you have no choice, Mr O'Brien. You can't register your ownership of the land otherwise.'

'I've never heard the like of it. I bet if Tyrone Power was here he wouldn't be looking for any social security numbers off of me.'

'I'm afraid he'd have to. It's the law, Mr O'Brien. You're not being singled out.'

'Well, in that case, I'm going to be reporting you both to the Law Society. This is outrageous carry-on.' He stood up shakily.

'You do that, Mr O'Brien.'

He glared at me and shuffled out of the room, mumbling to himself as he went.

Well, that was a good start.

At about 4.30, I heard more voices outside and Patricia poked her head around the door again.

'Are you ready for more clients?'

'Do they have an appointment?' I knew that I was wasting my breath.

'Well, no, but….'

'Sure. Show them in.' It couldn't go any worse than the last time.

Patricia ushered in what I could only describe as two sweet old ladies. They were wearing matching woollen berets and carrying matching square handbags.

'Please come in and take a seat, ladies.'

They both sat down, placing matching handbags on matching laps. Their smiles were focused on me, full beam.

'I'm Lainey Malone.'

'I'm Cissy Walsh, and this is my sister Hannah,' the old woman on the right said in a sweet, wavering, old-lady voice.

I took down their names. Sisters. I should have guessed. I wouldn't have been surprised to hear that they were twins – although it was hard to tell with old ladies, especially when they wore such similar hairstyles and clothes.

'And can I have your addresses, please?'

'We both live at the post office, Low Street, Ballyknock.' Cissy appeared to be the elected spokeswoman.

'Oh, do you run the post office, then?'

'That we do, and our parents before us,' said Cissy proudly. 'And where are you from, Miss Malone?'

'Oh, call me Lainey, please. I'm from Dublin.'

'Isn't that lovely. And are you going to be with us in Ballyknock for long?'

'Just for a few months, until Mr Power can get down.'

'Tyrone is a lovely man, isn't he?'

'You know him well, then?'

'Indeed and I do. Didn't I use to dandle him on my knee when he was still in nappies? His mother, God rest her, was a great friend of ours.'

I had a vision of Tyrone, wearing an adult diaper, sitting on Cissy's lap, squashing her and her handbag to death. I tried not to laugh.

Hannah still hadn't said a word, but, judging by her smile, she too thought that Tyrone was a lovely man.

'Have you been working for him long?'

'For about seven years. Now, what can I do for you today?'

The two women exchanged glances, their smiles faltering for a fraction of a second.

'Not a thing, my dear,' Cissy replied.

I was confused. 'Then why ...'

'We just wanted to come and introduce ourselves.'

'Oh. But I was asking you for your details....'

'Is that what you were doing?' Cissy laughed. 'We thought you were just being friendly. We had to come, you see. People will be coming into the post office asking about the new solicitor, so we had to come and find out for ourselves. Don't worry' – she positively twinkled at me – 'we'll be recommending you to everybody. You're very good.'

'But I haven't done anything.'

'You're a lovely girl – isn't she, Hannah?'

Hannah's smile seemed to agree that, yes, I was indeed a lovely girl.

'We won't take up any more of your time. You must be busy. I'm sure we'll be seeing you in the post office very soon. Goodbye now, and God bless.'

And they left.

Was it time to go home yet?

hed Jack furtively as he expertly built up
As he squatted in front of the wood-burner,
d for bum cleavage while pretending to
milk in the fridge. His overalls had been
by relatively clean jeans and a navy fleece.
wn, wavy hair was as tousled as before. I
hat his eyes were an intense bluey-green:
n's eyes, I thought. As I fussed around the
organising tea and biccies, I realised that
ly masculine presence in the house made
ll feminine and fluffy. The big strong man
from a day's physical labour, bringing fuel
ire. The man stokes the flames while the
prepares the food. I was disturbed by how
lt. *Call yourself a feminist?* Maybe he had
rts I could iron.

time at all, the fire blazed triumphantly in
th and I settled down gratefully before it;
temperature had dropped several degrees
ny impromptu nap. Jack sat down beside
e two-seater. Did he have to sit so close? I
arrassed by my proximity to this man, who
face it, a total stranger. I crossed my legs
om him and tugged involuntarily at my
make sure that it covered my knees. He
unabashed by the physical closeness –
to be relishing it, even. He grinned at me
eld the uncapped whiskey bottle above
;.
when.' He started to pour.

Chapter Seven

It was with sweet relief that I entered the front door of Power's Cottage that evening.

And then I thought of the rats.

The first thing that caught my eye was a scruffy note on the kitchen table. It was scrawled on the back of an old delivery docket.

Vermin dealt with. Shouldn't have any more trouble. Have filled in all obvious points of entry. Traps set in attic. Radar deterrents in all rooms. Call me if any more problems. Invoice sent to Tyrone Power & Co. in Dublin.

S. Murphy

Nice one! Thank you, Mr Rat-Catcher (excuse me – Mr Pest-Controller). I could kiss you!

What was that about radar deterrents? I looked around the room and spotted a strange, grey plastic object plugged into the wall. Patricia had told me about these earlier on: they emitted a high-pitched noise, which humans couldn't hear, but which was meant to drive rodents insane and send them packing. On further inspection I discovered that there was one in every room, including the bedroom. Relieved, I threw myself onto the bed.

I was awoken some time later by a loud knocking noise. I sat bolt upright on the bed. My initial thought was that the rats had returned with a vengeance. Then I realised that someone was knocking on the front door.

A visitor? For me?

Who could it be?

It was dark outside. The clock said nine. I got up and searched groggily for my shoes, which were exactly where I had kicked them – one underneath the wardrobe and the other on top of the blanket box. I slipped them on and adjusted my skirt, which was back to front.

I could see through the glass that there was a man at the door. I didn't recognise the back that was presented to me. Perhaps it was Billy the Axe Murderer.

'Hello, who's there?'

My visitor turned
recognised that broa
smiled his devastatin
'Oh, come in, Jack
Jack was laden d
'The mother sent m
reckoned you'd be c
thought I should wa
Did he mean to b
filthy mind?
'That was very ni
down here.' I gesture
wood-burner. He unl
to face me, massive h
out of breath.
'Well, what do I g
flirtatiously.
Anything you like.
'Would you like a
England couldn't have
'Cup of tea would
I even brought somet
He reached into his
of Toffee Pops I'd b
bottle of Paddy emerg
'Do you always car
with you?'
He winked. 'Only
kettle on, girl, and I'll
Seemed like a good

I wat
the fire.
I check
check fo
replaced
His bro
noticed
Fisherm
kitchen,
his over
me feel
comes i
for the
woman
nice it
some sh
In no
the hea
my bod
due to
me on
felt emb
was, let
away fi
skirt to
seemed
seemed
as he
my mu
'Say

Chapter Seven

It was with sweet relief that I entered the front door of Power's Cottage that evening.

And then I thought of the rats.

The first thing that caught my eye was a scruffy note on the kitchen table. It was scrawled on the back of an old delivery docket.

Vermin dealt with. Shouldn't have any more trouble. Have filled in all obvious points of entry. Traps set in attic. Radar deterrents in all rooms. Call me if any more problems. Invoice sent to Tyrone Power & Co. in Dublin.

S. Murphy

Nice one! Thank you, Mr Rat-Catcher (excuse me – Mr Pest-Controller). I could kiss you!

What was that about radar deterrents? I looked around the room and spotted a strange, grey plastic object plugged into the wall. Patricia had told me about these earlier on: they emitted a high-pitched noise, which humans couldn't hear, but which was meant to drive rodents insane and send them packing. On further inspection I discovered that there was one in every room, including the bedroom. Relieved, I threw myself onto the bed.

I was awoken some time later by a loud knocking noise. I sat bolt upright on the bed. My initial thought was that the rats had returned with a vengeance. Then I realised that someone was knocking on the front door.

A visitor? For me?

Who could it be?

It was dark outside. The clock said nine. I got up and searched groggily for my shoes, which were exactly where I had kicked them – one underneath the wardrobe and the other on top of the blanket box. I slipped them on and adjusted my skirt, which was back to front.

I could see through the glass that there was a man at the door. I didn't recognise the back that was presented to me. Perhaps it was Billy the Axe Murderer.

'Hello, who's there?'

My visitor turned around. How could I not have recognised that broad expanse of back? Jack Power smiled his devastating smile, and I was devastated.

'Oh, come in, Jack!' I simpered. (*Stop simpering!*)

Jack was laden down with an armful of logs. 'The mother sent me with wood for the fire. She reckoned you'd be cold, up here in the hills. She thought I should warm you up.'

Did he mean to be suggestive, or was it just my filthy mind?

'That was very nice of her. You can put them down here.' I gestured to a free corner beside the wood-burner. He unburdened himself and turned to face me, massive hands on narrow hips, slightly out of breath.

'Well, what do I get for my trouble?' He smiled flirtatiously.

Anything you like.

'Would you like a cup of tea?' The Queen of England couldn't have been more proper.

'Cup of tea would go down nicely, thanks. And I even brought something to go with it.'

He reached into his pocket. Instead of the packet of Toffee Pops I'd been expecting, a mostly-full bottle of Paddy emerged. Yippee!

'Do you always carry a bottle of whiskey around with you?'

He winked. 'Only for special occasions. Put the kettle on, girl, and I'll get this fire going.'

Seemed like a good trade.

I watched Jack furtively as he expertly built up the fire. As he squatted in front of the wood-burner, I checked for bum cleavage while pretending to check for milk in the fridge. His overalls had been replaced by relatively clean jeans and a navy fleece. His brown, wavy hair was as tousled as before. I noticed that his eyes were an intense bluey-green: *Fisherman's eyes*, I thought. As I fussed around the kitchen, organising tea and biccies, I realised that his overtly masculine presence in the house made me feel all feminine and fluffy. The big strong man comes in from a day's physical labour, bringing fuel for the fire. The man stokes the flames while the woman prepares the food. I was disturbed by how nice it felt. *Call yourself a feminist?* Maybe he had some shirts I could iron.

In no time at all, the fire blazed triumphantly in the hearth and I settled down gratefully before it; my body temperature had dropped several degrees due to my impromptu nap. Jack sat down beside me on the two-seater. Did he have to sit so close? I felt embarrassed by my proximity to this man, who was, let's face it, a total stranger. I crossed my legs away from him and tugged involuntarily at my skirt to make sure that it covered my knees. He seemed unabashed by the physical closeness – seemed to be relishing it, even. He grinned at me as he held the uncapped whiskey bottle above my mug.

'Say when.' He started to pour.